LEO
saves VENICE

STORY BY ALBERTO TOSO FEI
ILLUSTRATED BY YANSU WANG

lineadacqua

Story by
Alberto Toso Fei

Translation
Lucian Comoy

Illustrations
Yansu Wang

Graphic design
Ludovica Taddeo

Editorial coordination
Francesca Ortalli

© InnoVe
© lineadacqua
© Yansu Wang

*In our heart, we all have
our own courageous Knight, ever
ready to set off on a new quest.*

Gianni Rodari, *Don Quixote*

Leo is a cat. But not just any cat, for Leo is a Venetian cat.
No one knows where he came from, nor where his family is from,
although it is said to be very far away, somewhere in the Orient.
He has no owner; his home is the city. He has many friends:
the keeper of the Doge's Palace, the fishmonger at the Rialto
and, above all, his little mouse friends. Not to mention Mr C,
the cormorant, with whom Leo stops to chat on the rooftops;
they often go for acrobatic flights
in the Venetian skies.
Leo loves being on the rooftops
because… he doesn't like water.
Like all cats, he's afraid of it;
how strange for a cat who
lives in a city full of canals!

Here he is, as with one leap
he jumps on Mr C's back
and flies towards the Grand Canal
and another friend, Teo the gondolier,
who hears his meowing and looks up:
'Ciao Leo!'
'*Miaow!*' replies Leo in cat fashion.
Teo is a man, of course,
and cannot understand him.
'Look how good you look
in that little gondolier uniform
I sewed for you...'
'*Miaow, miaow!*' – thank you, I'm so happy –
Leo replies again, and in a flash he grabs
the gondolier's hat.
'*Miaooow!*' – I'm only borrowing it! –
yells the cat as Mr C flies off
in the blink of an eye.

Leo is very happy in Venice
and really loves his city.
That is why he does not hesitate
to invite Venetians and visitors
to behave respectfully:
not to leave litter, of course.
But also not to sit on the bridges
and so make it difficult for the elderly
to get by, or leave food lying around.
People usually welcome Leo's suggestions.

Sometimes, instead,
rubbish dropped by people
mysteriously finds its way
back into its owners' bags…
But these are very rare cases:
everyone loves Venice!

So, is everything OK? Hmmm…
Leo does have one worry:
his name is Mr G,
and he's a seagull; together
with his allies, the rats,
he rages through the city,
plundering all the food he can,
sometimes even stealing it
from people's hands.
He never seems to have enough.

And here he is, Mr G: he has just summoned the rats
to a dilapidated warehouse, headed by the fearsome Kurz,
the biggest and oldest rat in all of Venice.
'Yesterday I was in St Mark's Square,' says Mr G to Kurz,
'and I was standing on a windowsill of the Marciana Library,
one of the oldest in the world, waiting for some tourist to pass by
with a juicy sandwich to steal...'
'So what?' Kurz replied, 'We don't like books, they don't taste good'.
'Hang on! There was a scholar there reading about the existence
of a wind, held prisoner since time immemorial in the dungeons
of the Doge's Palace: its name is Scirocco.'
'I don't see what use it can be to us...' (Kurz doesn't have much
imagination.)
'If we free him, we can use him to bring us all the food we want,
all the food in town! But we'll need your little rodent hands
and your ability to creep through anything to find the cell
and open it.'

That very night
the rats quietly slip
into the Doge's Palace
and reach the dungeons.

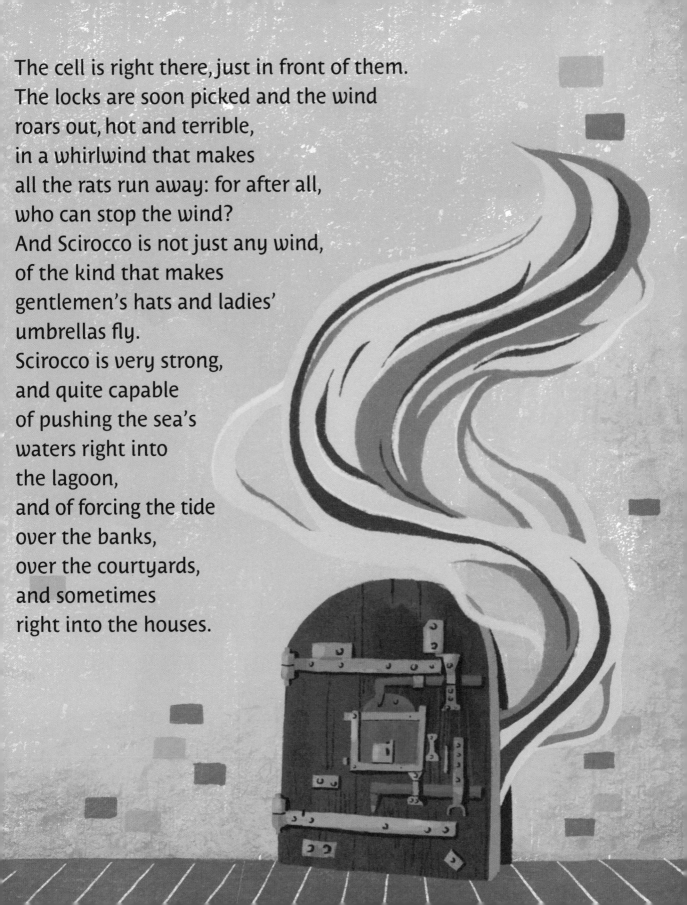

The cell is right there, just in front of them.
The locks are soon picked and the wind
roars out, hot and terrible,
in a whirlwind that makes
all the rats run away: for after all,
who can stop the wind?
And Scirocco is not just any wind,
of the kind that makes
gentlemen's hats and ladies'
umbrellas fly.
Scirocco is very strong,
and quite capable
of pushing the sea's
waters right into
the lagoon,
and of forcing the tide
over the banks,
over the courtyards,
and sometimes
right into the houses.

Mr G and the other seagulls are also thrown about all over the place
as he blows by. They had deluded themselves that the wind
might be their ally, but now they're scared stiff;
the rats have come out of their warrens, which are underwater now,
and the water continues to rise, rise, rise... oh so high!

The wind whistles through the gondolas
and makes them bang together.
Teo tries to make sure his is safe,
while the fishmonger moves the boxes
with the fish into his warehouse,
and the keeper of the Doge's Palace
bolts a panel in front of the main
door to stop the water
from getting in.

Meanwhile, Leo and the little mice
fly fearlessly through the turbulent air
astride Mr C and his pigeon friends.
The wind scares them,
but there are so many people to help!
Our Leo and his companions
stop at the shop of a maker
of Venetian masks and help by
passing each other one mask at a time,
putting them somewhere safe and dry.

Leo continues his patrol,
and then he sees a little girl
coming out of a door chasing her doll
which is floating in the water.
Her Mum and Dad haven't noticed
anything, as they're busy
saving the family's belongings.
The girl takes a few steps and...
SPLASH!, ends up in the canal.
She's in danger.
Leo has no hesitation:
he dives in to help her.
But he has forgotten one thing:
he can't swim!

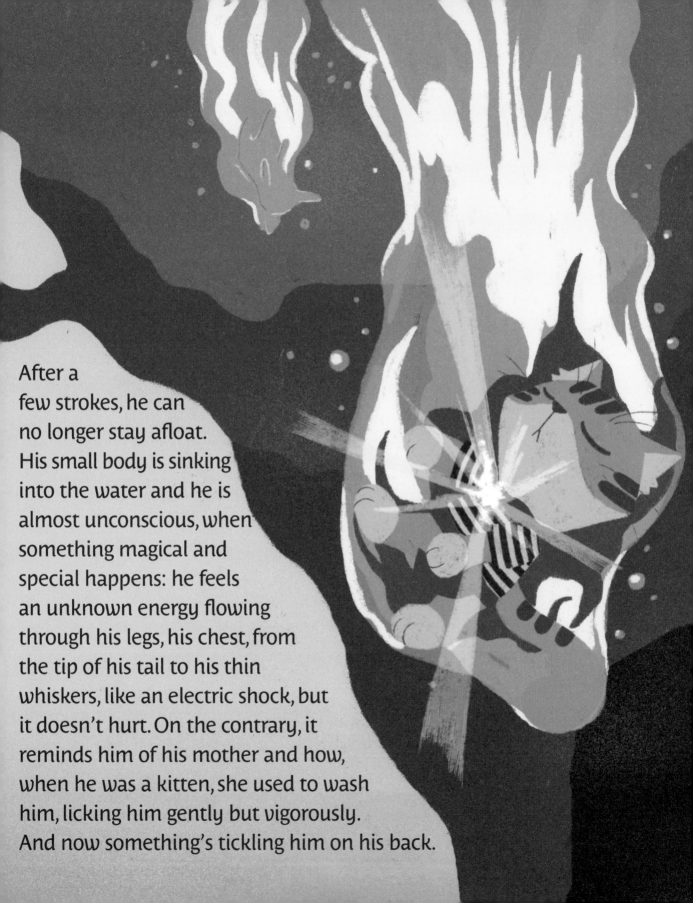

After a
few strokes, he can
no longer stay afloat.
His small body is sinking
into the water and he is
almost unconscious, when
something magical and
special happens: he feels
an unknown energy flowing
through his legs, his chest, from
the tip of his tail to his thin
whiskers, like an electric shock, but
it doesn't hurt. On the contrary, it
reminds him of his mother and how,
when he was a kitten, she used to wash
him, licking him gently but vigorously.
And now something's tickling him on his back.

Leo opens his eyes:
his body has changed!
He has become
a mighty lion with wings,
the very symbol of Venice.
How could this happen?
But there is no time to ask questions,
because the girl is still in danger.
With two strokes
the new Leo reaches her
and then he takes off,
strong and fast.

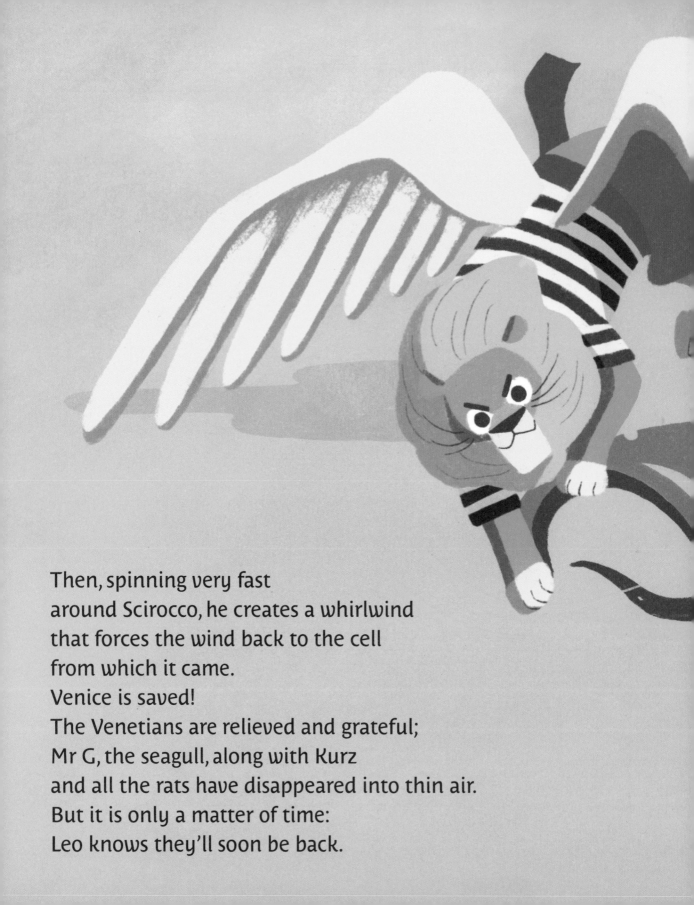

Then, spinning very fast
around Scirocco, he creates a whirlwind
that forces the wind back to the cell
from which it came.
Venice is saved!
The Venetians are relieved and grateful;
Mr G, the seagull, along with Kurz
and all the rats have disappeared into thin air.
But it is only a matter of time:
Leo knows they'll soon be back.

Now Leo flies to St Mark's Column, where another winged lion has been watching the sea and the Orient for centuries.
The little mice join him, astonished.
'Is it really you?', they ask him admiringly.
'Yes, something magical has happened, but it's still me', he replies.
'Look, he's turning into our Leo again!', says a mouse, pointing with a tiny finger, and Leo realises that he will soon be a cat again.
But he also knows that all he has to do is renew the water magic whenever the city needs it.

Meanwhile, he will have plenty of time to learn
something more of his story. Who is he really?
What are his origins? But he will also have time
for fun and to play with his friends
in the most beautiful city in the world:
Venice.

To be continued…

lineadacqua edizioni *for* InnoVe
San Marco 3716/b
30124 Venezia
www.lineadacqua.com

Printed by Grafiche Veneziane, Venice

First edition March 2022
First reprint May 2022

ISBN 979-12-809-7901-8

made in venice

MIX
Paper from
responsible sources
FSC® C151617